On a Pirate Ship

Edited by Anna Milbourne.
With thanks to Richard Platt
for information about pirates.

First published in 2007 by Usborne Publishing Ltd.,
Usborne House, 83-85 Saffron Hill, London EC1N 8RT
England. usborne.com Copyright © 2007 Usborne Publishing
Ltd. The name Usborne and the devices are Trade
Marks of Usborne Publishing Ltd. All rights reserved. No part
of this publication may be reproduced, stored in a retrieval
system, or transmitted in any form or by any means, electronic,
mechanical, photocopying, recording or otherwise without the
prior permission of Usborne Publishing Ltd. First published
in America 2007. UE, EDC, Tulsa, Oklahoma 74146.
www.usbornebooksandmore.com.

On a Pirate Ship

Sarah Courtauld

Illustrated by Benji Davies

Designed by Laura Parker

Have you ever wondered
what it would be like
to live on a pirate ship?

Just imagine setting sail.

"All aboard!" the Captain shouts,
and everyone scrambles onto the ship.

The wind puffs into
the enormous sails...

...and pushes the ship
across the waves.

To steer, the Captain turns
the heavy wooden wheel.

By day, he follows his trusty maps.

By night, he follows the twinkling stars,
and the ship glides over the silent sea.

All at once, a wild wind roars and **giant waves** crash over the deck.

The wind begins to rip the sails,
so the pirates haul them in.

Everyone clings on for dear life
as the ship rides through the storm.

In the morning,
all is calm...

...and the pirates stitch up
the raggedy sails.

The youngest pirate climbs the mast
and spies a treasure ship.

"Ship
ahoy!"

"All hands on deck!"
the Captain cries.

Mile after mile,
across the sea,
the pirates chase
the treasure ship.

When they're close,
they fire the cannons.

BOOM!

They catch up with the ship and leap aboard.

AARGH!

They fight until
the battle's won.

...and hundreds and hundreds of gold doubloons.

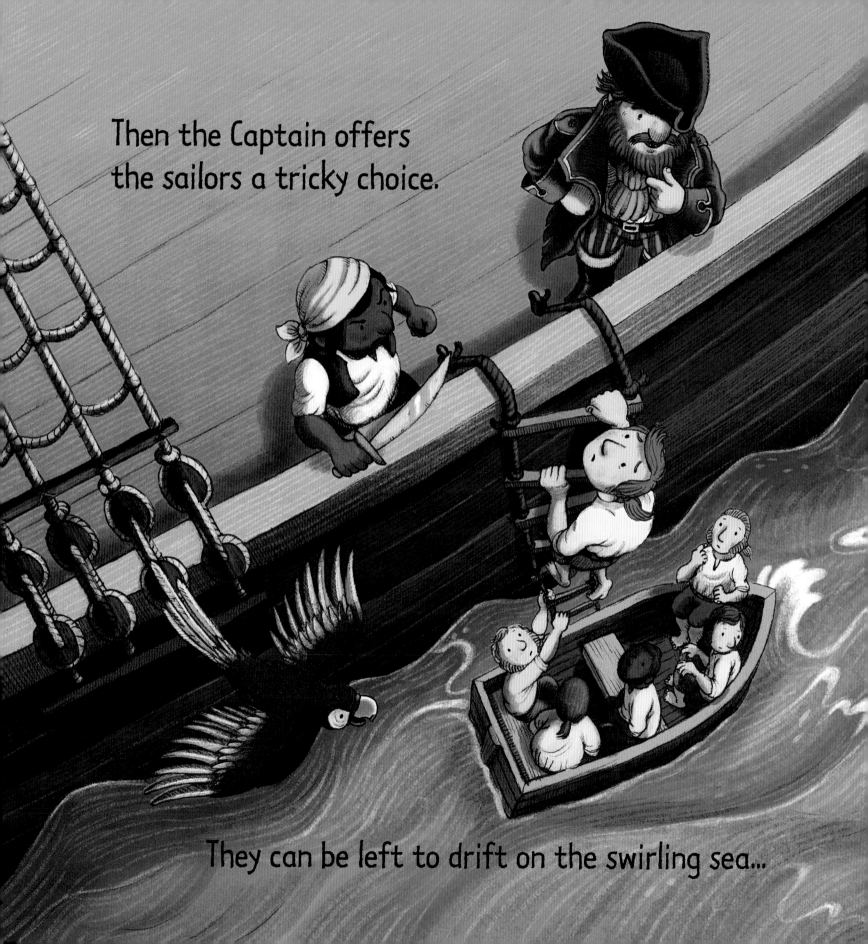

Then the Captain offers
the sailors a tricky choice.

They can be left to drift on the swirling sea...

...or they can join his fearless crew.

They decide to become pirates.

Everybody celebrates with hot, spicy drinks.

They dance until they're dizzy, and sing merry songs.

Suddenly, the Captain spies danger on the way.

If the pirates get caught with the treasure, they'll be in deep, deep trouble.

They race away
across the waves...

...and hide until
the coast is clear.

Soon they'll set sail
on their next adventure.

Do you think that you'd be brave enough to live on a pirate ship?